MINDMATTERS:
WHISPERS, WONDERS AND A LITTLE SOUL SEARCHING

ISBN: 978-0-8819-3226-3
Edited by: Glory Abah
Designed by: Coker-Prempeh Olamide
Printed by: Printserve
Publisher: Emphaloz Publishing House
For inquiries,permissions,or speaking engagements, please write to enquiries@mindmatters.ng

Dedicated to Ms Mo, Dearest Feng & My Demi!

For the overthinkers, the feel-everythingers, and the "I'll just write it down instead" crew.

This book gets you.

Also dedicated to everyone who cheered me on, corrected my commas, & reminded me I had something worth saying.
Mentors, this one's on your report card too.

Some people make noise. Others make meaning. Buzz, true to her name, does the latter. From the moment she stepped into my world, I was struck by her hum - not loud, but constant; not boastful, but impossible to ignore. That's how the nickname came to be: Buzz. It fit perfectly - not just because of her boundless energy, but because of everything she reminded me of in the bee. Funmilayo Falola is who I fondly refer to as Buzz with a few more zzzzzs as two zzs wouldn't be enough to adequately capture her essence.

Bees are often underestimated. Diminutive, almost delicate. But in truth, they are essential - holding together the delicate balance of our biosphere with quiet persistence. They are engineers of ecosystems, invisible linchpins of abundance. Without them, flowers would not bloom, crops would not thrive, and life as we know it would unravel.

Buzz embodies this same kind of impact. She moves with intention, gathers meaning from even the smallest moments, and somehow leaves behind a trail of insight and connection, pollinating minds and souls in ways most don't even realize at first. Her energy is vibrant, but her work is deeply rooted. She doesn't seek attention, but she certainly commands respect.

And like the bee's distinct golden stripes, Buzz has her own signature flourish - a love for bold, colourful shoes that announce her presence with a joyful defiance, a burst of brightness against the grayscale of the everyday.

This book, Mind Matters: Whispers, wonders and a Little Soul Searching is her hive; crafted from moments of reflection, discipline, vulnerability, and a genuine hunger for purpose. The opening section, Whispers of My Soul sets the tone beautifully, not as a shout for attention, but as a gentle call inward. These musings carry weight not because they're grand, but because they're honest. And honesty, like pollen, spreads life when carried with care.

I've been privileged to watch the author grow into someone who doesn't just think deeply but lives deliberately. Someone who, like the bee, makes everything around her a little more alive, a little more in bloom. And this book, tender, thoughtful, quietly radiant, is her gift to us.
So, I invite you to read slowly. Listen closely. Let her words move through you like wings in motion. There is much to learn from the bee, and from the author, who has captured its spirit in every page.
This collection doesn't demand to be understood, it only asks to be felt. Let it guide you where it must.

Folakemi Ani-Mumuney (FAM)

INTRODUCTION

WHISPERS OF MY SOUL

Alright, here we go. Life is a wild ride, right? One minute you're sipping your tea like a civilised human, and the next, you're spilling it all over yourself because you tripped on nothing. Nothing! I mean, how does that even happen? Life can hit you with a series of unexpected plot twists, like you're just trying to get through your to-do list and suddenly bam-the universe throws a wrench in your plans, and you're left juggling too many balls, a half-finished cup of tea, and a mild existential crisis.

But here's the thing: we're all just winging it. If you think everyone else has their life perfectly together and you're the only one stumbling, let me just say-nope, you're not alone. We're all living in a state of beautiful, messy chaos, and somehow, we're still getting through it. We may not always have it together (spoiler alert: I definitely don't), but we can at least try to figure it out with a little grace - and a lot of humour.

This book is my collection of life's musings. It's me, pouring my thoughts, my randomness, and my messiness into these pages. You'll find reflections on life's ups, downs, and all the in-betweens. It's about the times I've gotten knocked down and then, like a badly coordinated toddler, I've somehow gotten back up, half smiling, strained and tired, tea stains all over my shirt, but nonetheless still standing. How can I be both a hot and a hopeful mess at the same time? How can I be completely vulnerable one minute and then crack jokes the next, laughing at and with myself? All the while, I'm clinging to God and praying He doesn't let me fall flat in this thing called life.

Let's be clear: I'm not here to pretend like I have it all figured out. If you're hoping for a polished, self-help guru kind of vibe, you're probably in the wrong place. But if you're looking for someone who understands that life is messy, funny, frustrating, and sometimes feels like trying to fold fitted sheets (how do we even do that?), then welcome. You're in the right spot.

There's no perfect answer to how we navigate life's crazy ride, but I do know one thing: grace is a game-changer. It's that little nudge from the universe (or, in my case, from God) that whispers, "You got this," even when you feel like you don't. And here's a fun little secret - sometimes a hot cup of tea is the answer too. Grace and tea. It's my combo for surviving it all, one messy moment at a time.

So whether you're juggling twelve things, tripping over life's curveballs, or just trying to survive the day, know that you're not alone. We're all just figuring it out as we go along - falling, laughing, picking ourselves up again, and moving forward with a bit of grace (and maybe a lot of humor).

So grab your cup, sit back, and let's laugh at this crazy ride together. Because life is not perfect, and neither are we - but we're still here, still trying, and we've got grace on our side.

Let's do this!

CHARACTER, DISCIPLINE & OTHER MUSINGS

What moments have you been experiencing lately

(Be honest... was it deep... or just you arguing with a mosquito at 2am instead of facing your emotions)

Read the text on the other page, then come back here to confess.

We're all friends, liars, and emotionally unstable geniuses here.

AH, **MOMENTS.**

Where do I even start? Honestly, if you tell me you don't love moments, I might just side-eye you and quietly back away, because moments are my thing. Forget fireworks, the accolades or waiting to be crowned "Employee of the Month." Me, I live for the tiny, soul-warming, mess-up-and-try-again kind of moments.

I see people chasing the big, loud wins, the ones that come with confetti, champagne, and a perfectly timed victory speech (you know, the kind that gets one million views on TikTok), and there is nothing wrong with that!

Me, I'm over here, sipping my tea and giving a thumbs up to the little things, like that weird little dance you do when you find your keys after searching for them in the most chaotic, frantic way possible. That's a moment. A glorious, underrated moment. It's also in the small sighs-those little "finally, I can breathe" moments when you kick your shoes off, take off your bra, and flop on the couch like a pancake after a long day. You just lay there, pretending you're in a wellness commercial, but secretly wondering how your life turned into a never-ending loop of "what's for dinner?" Those are the moments that are worth everything 😊

But here's the thing I LOVE about moments: they're not always perfect, and I'm totally okay with that. I mean, if life were perfect, where would the fun be? The real magic is in the trying. That awkward moment when you try something new and it goes horribly wrong-like cooking a new recipe and ending up with something that looks like an abstract painting rather than food. But hey, you tried!

It's like life is this giant "trial and error" class, and we're all just out here getting an "A" for effort, right?
And don't even get me started on falling down and getting back up. Falling is a moment. Sometimes, I like to think of it as life's way of making me do the cha-cha-cha. Fall. Get up. Shake it off. Fall again. Try again. And yes, maybe I look a bit ridiculous, but who's watching? Just me, living my best "didn't get it right, but I'll try a thousand more times" life. LOL.

The truth is, we spend way too much time waiting for life's "big moments," like when you finally get that promotion, get that big break, or you win that game. But honestly, that's just the icing on the cake. What really makes up the cake are the little, quirky moments we forget to notice: the accidental pun that cracks you up, the awkward but heartwarming hug from a friend, the laughter you enjoy with friends, the tears cried in private, or when you're dancing like nobody's watching - except you hope they are, because it's a vibe.

So yeah, I adore moments! Not the loud ones that everyone's waiting for, but the messy, funny, sometimes embarrassing moments that happen when no one's looking. They count. They matter. And if anyone tries to tell you that chasing them is silly, just remember: you're living for the moments they'll never understand. Keep collecting them. Because I've got a pretty solid collection going, and I wouldn't trade it for all the confetti in the world.
Cheers to the moments ahead

Now go back to the other page to share some of your moments!

MOMENTS MATTER

The promotions. The product launches. The big wins.
They're loud. Visible. Enjoyable. Shareable.
But lately, I've been thinking about moments.
The quiet ones. The in-between ones. The ones that don't make the highlight reel, but somehow leave a mark.

The moment you chose to try again.
The moment someone truly saw you.
The moment you said no, when you used to say yes.
The moment something clicked - internally - long before you saw it externally.

These are the moments that shift us. That stretch us. That transform us.
We talk so much about goals and outcomes (and those matter).
But let's not lose sight of the journey.

Of the intentionality and authenticity we carry through it.
Because sometimes, the real victories aren't in the destination, they are in who we become along the way.
So here's to the moments.
The small ones. The brave ones. The ones that change everything, quietly.

LIVING WITH INTENTION

I don't have it all figured out - like, not at all.
Some days I wake up ready to drink green juice and make empowered choices like a boss lady. Other days, I accidentally eat chocolate for breakfast and wonder how I became emotionally dependent on voice notes and drinking tea.

But somewhere in between all that, I've started trying to live more intentionally. And with purpose. Not because I'm suddenly enlightened, but because... I kind of had to.
Life has this sneaky way of moving really fast while making you feel like you're standing still. You wake up, do the things, tick the boxes, nod in the Zoom calls, and before you know it, you're like, "Wait. Is this... it?"

I had that moment - more than once - where I looked around at the life I was living and it seemed I didn't really choose half of it. I just kind of... went along with it. Like I was letting the algorithm decide my life.
So I started paying attention. Slowly. Awkwardly. Without a plan.

I started asking myself: Does this feel like me? Am I doing this because I want to or because I think I should? Is this actually making me happy, or do I just like how it looks on the outside?

And let me tell you - intentional living isn't glamorous.
Sometimes it looks like saying no to things that used to feel like the highlight reel. Sometimes it looks like not knowing what comes next, but trusting yourself enough to let something go anyway. Sometimes it looks like staying in on a Friday night and having deep thoughts in your PJs like a melodramatic playlist with no skip button.
It's been uncomfortable. Also weirdly freeing. Also a bit chaotic. But somewhere in that mess, I started finding myself again.

Then came the purposeful part.
Not the grand, "change the world" kind of purpose -
but the gentle kind.
Like, "What actually matters to me?"
What kind of life feels honest? What kind of people make me feel at home? What are the things I want to look back on and say, "Yes, that was worth it."

I still don't have a 5-year plan. I barely have a 5-day one.
But I know I want to be present.
I want to mean what I say.
I want to stop auto-piloting through the days like they're just things to survive.
So no, I haven't nailed it. I'm still very much winging it. Yup! Winging it, but with intention.
I'm winging it on purpose.
And honestly? That feels like a good place to start.

PURPOSE… OR JUST EXPENSIVE CONFUSION IN CUTE SHOES?

I love shoes.
Not the practical, everyday ones.
No - I love the loud ones. The shoes that look like they have opinions. The type that makes people stop and stare like, "Who told her this was okay?" And I proudly wear them, because they make me smile.
But finding them? It's a mission. You comb markets, scroll endlessly online, ask your plug if there's any new stock.

Funny how that reminds me of how we talk about finding purpose.
Like it's on a shelf in a display window somewhere next to that one perfect pair of shoes: expensive, dramatic, and confusing - and by the way, it's got a tag that says "Destiny," so you buy it anyway.

We are told - Find your purpose!
As if it's hiding in a dusty corner in a supermarket or Yaba market or even in-between church vigils and vision board nights.

Honestly, I'm learning that purpose isn't something we stumble into - it's something we show up for.
It's not about a title, a stage, or a viral moment.
It's not always loud.
Sometimes, it's quiet - a soft whisper in the chaos.
It's showing up. Living true. Living fully.
Purpose is presence.

It's in the now.
It's in the life I'm living at the pace of grace - not hustle, not hype, but alignment.
It's walking with God - sometimes boldly, sometimes wobbling in over-the-top heels; but walking still.
It's in the small things, the sacred, the mundane.
It's me, being faithful in what looks ordinary, but knowing God is weaving something extraordinary.

So no, I don't have a five-year plan, a boss lady map, or a conquer the world frame on my wall.
And on some days I may look like chaos in sequins.
But I'm not lost.
I'm not aimless.

And these shoes? They're not just for aesthetics - they're walking me in purpose, one quirky, intentional step at a time.
Because purpose isn't performance.
It's choosing kindness over sarcasm.
It's choosing peace when pettiness is waving like an usher at a revival.
It's sending that "You good?" message.
It's making space to laugh, cry, serve, and still leave room to be.
You don't need to build a global empire to be purposeful.
Sometimes, just being here is proof enough that you're on purpose.

And yes - even in the wildest pair of shoes in your wardrobe.

FIND YOUR PURPOSE…
THEY SAID

You hunted purpose like it was on sale,
Displayed behind glass with angelic lighting,
Labelled: "Divine Calling - Last One, Size Elusive."
Right next to a pair of painfully expensive shoes
That look like they'll ruin your ankles,
But everyone insists are "so you."

You thought purpose would arrive like a Netflix prophecy-
Loud, glowing, dramatic.
A voice from the heavens… or at least a WhatsApp broadcast.
Nope!
Purpose strolled in, unbothered,
Wearing socks and slippers,
Looking suspiciously at you like your regular Tuesday.

It turned out to be in your group chats,
Your awkward Zoom prayers,
Your almost-burnt dinner for a friend.
In the "God, I'm tired but okay, let's do this anyway" moments.

You thought it would be red carpets and revelations.
But it's more like remembering to call your mum,
Holding your tongue (again),
And saying "God bless you" when what you really wanted
to say needed censoring.
Purpose isn't about being perfect.
It's showing up.
Stumbling sometimes. Still moving.
This moment, this unfiltered, Wi-Fi-buffering version of you
Yup, that's still purpose.

It's not lost.
It's not late.
It's just vibing in your favorite pair of chaotic, colorful
shoes.
The ones nobody understands…
Yet, they walk just right.

Dream Big
find your why
who am i?
purpose

LET'S TALK ABOUT DISCIPLINE.

You know that mythical unicorn trait everyone on podcasts, TED Talks, and "momfluencers" with four color-coded calendars swear by.
Meanwhile, I'm just over here with two teenagers, a half-filled planner that looks like it's been through hell, and a tea mug that mysteriously keeps disappearing (because apparently, teenagers need mugs now too).

For years, I thought discipline was about hustle. Routines. Alarms. Green juices. Salads. Waking up at dawn with perfect skin and a beautiful smile.
Spoiler alert: I wake up at 5 a.m. to jog, and I still look like I lost a fight to my duvet.
Despite my love for a good snooze button, I've stuck with it.
And I've seen the results - 10kg down, a bit more strength in my thighs and my mindset.
Not because I became someone else.
But because I became more faithful to me.

See, ehn, discipline isn't about being perfect.
It's about being consistent, even when your life feels like a never-ending group chat of teen sarcasm, work deadlines, boring meetings, and grocery lists that somehow never include what you actually need. It's about choosing not to scroll for two hours while avoiding a conversation with your 16-year-old who suddenly has thoughts about life and clothes at midnight. Saying no to another unnecessary Zoom meeting because your 13-year-old wants help with something that may or may not be math. Showing up for your team with kindness, even when you're running on chai, fumes, and passive-aggressive Post-it notes.

And boundaries?
Oh, honey. They are discipline in glittery disguise. It's saying *no* when you've got nothing left to give, not having to explain yourself to everyone and their group chats. It's saying *yes* when you know it's a stretch, but it aligns with what really matters. It's teaching your teens that you're a whole human being, not just their ride, their ATM card, Wi-Fi provider, or their emotional sponge.

And vulnerability? That's discipline too.
It's admitting, "I'm tired." It's letting others support you instead of holding everything like you're a one-woman show (with teenagers?... let's be real, you kind of are 😊). It's being *okay* with slow progress and celebrating it like it's a Grammy.
So, what does discipline look like for me now?
It's hiding in the bathroom just to breathe (without anyone asking, "What's for dinner?").
It's choosing to be present instead of productive all the time.
It's leading my work team like I lead my home: with boundaries, humor, a little prayer, and snacks.

Discipline isn't always pretty.
Sometimes, it's dragging yourself out of bed before the sun rises to jog in leggings older than your 13-year-old. Resisting the urge to reply to that *one* spicy work email with equal spice (deep breaths, deep breaths). Saying "no" to chaos and "yes" to peace, even if peace looks like ignoring laundry and lighting a candle in your room like it's a spa retreat. And sometimes... it's just finding both socks and not stepping on a LEGO.
Discipline is in the choosing, the showing up.
Socks, sarcasm, and all.

STILL ON DISCIPLINE

Discipline is not glamorous, it's rarely in gold,
It's doing the boring when you'd rather be bold.
It's lacing your running shoes at five-oh-five,
When your bed is whispering, "Don't you dare strive."
It's meal-prepped Sundays, not fries on the go,
It's budgeting wisely when the shops scream, "Hello!"
It's texts you don't send, the sass you resist,
The grace you extend when you'd rather throw fists.

It's quiet commitment, a whisper, not a shout,
The slow, sacred yes to what life is all about.
It's messy and real, it's showing up still,
Not always with sparkle, but always with will.
So here's to the small steps, the unseen fights,
The daily decision to walk in the light.
Not perfect, not fancy, not free of all sin,
But faithful, consistent...That's discipline.

THIS IS A SAFE SPACE FOR TRUTH, DELUSION, AND DRAMATIC SELF-DISCOVERY.

Fill in the bubbles with your most authentic self.
Your inner child is watching.

BEING AUTHENTIC ISN'T ALWAYS CUTE.

Let's just start there.
Everyone says, "Be yourself!" like it's this sparkly, Instagrammable thing. But the truth is, being yourself - your full, unfiltered, slightly chaotic, beautiful mess of a self - can feel terrifying. Like "Did I just say that out loud?" kind of terrifying, uhn!
I try to be authentic. Actually, not try - I am authentic!

This is me. No mask. No fake voice. No pretending to love things I don't. I laugh out loud. I ask real questions. I show up with my whole heart, even when I don't know how it's going to land.
But sometimes I look around and think...
Do people even like that? Because it often feels like the world prefers curated over real.
Perfect hair, filtered skin, polished captions, rehearsed vibes.
Fake bags. Fake smiles. Fake deep.
And here I am, just showing up as myself, wondering if I missed some secret meeting where everyone agreed to pretend.

I have these moments, these mini spirals where I ask myself:

Why am I like this?
Why can't I just blend in?
Did I overshare?
Was I too much?
Did I say the wrong thing again?
Do they think I'm weird?
Do they think I'm... too different?
And then the worst one: why don't they like me?

Phew. That one stings. Because being authentic means you're putting your real self out there, not the version you know they'll clap for. So when you feel rejected, it's not just your image being rejected: it's you, all of you. That's what makes it hard. That's what makes it vulnerable.

But here's what I keep reminding myself:
Yes, I'm different. Yes, I'm not for everyone.
But the people who get me, the ones who see me and don't flinch — they are the ones that matter. I don't want to twist myself into a version easier to swallow. I've done that before. It felt safe, but it never felt like home.
And don't get me wrong: authenticity isn't perfection.

It doesn't mean I have it all figured out. I don't.
I mess up, overspeak, overthink, laugh at the wrong times, get scared, and get insecure.
But I'm also learning to hold space for that, to be bold in who I am while still growing, healing, and learning how to show up better.

Authenticity doesn't mean staying the same forever. It means being true, even in your becoming. Even when you're unsure, even when you're scared they won't clap, even when you don't get the validation, the approval, the likes.
So yes, I'm still figuring it out. Still wondering sometimes if I'm too much, or not enough.
Still catching myself thinking, "Why can't I just be like everyone else?" But I also know I was never meant to be.

That could be the whole point.
To be real, even when it's scary.
To be soft, even when it would be easier to be silent.
To be me, even if I shake while doing it.
Because this world has enough fake.
Enough surface. Enough "perfect." But the real stuff? That's rare. That's brave.
That's me.

OHHH, FRIENDSHIP, I TIRE!

You know, they don't warn you about friendship being one of the most beautiful, complicated, sometimes exhausting, often hilarious, and deeply emotional parts of being human. They tell you about romantic love, heartbreak, success, even failure - but friendship? That one sneaks up on you.
Because phew, this thing called friendship?
It will build you, break you, heal you, and sometimes have you lying in bed like,"Is it me? Am I the problem?"

There are seasons when friendship is pure magic: belly-laughs, inside jokes, late-night confessions, turning the worst days into something you can laugh about later. The kind of moments that remind you you're not alone. That someone gets you. That someone chooses you, not because they have to, but because they want to.

But then... there are other seasons.
The awkward drift, the unspoken tension, the "Are we still close or am I imagining this distance?" feeling, the ghosting, the weird power dynamics, the subtle competition, the "I showed up for you, but you didn't show up for me" ache.
Friendship is work.

It's not always matching energy - sometimes it's holding the space while the other person finds theirs. Sometimes it's forgiving people who never said sorry. Sometimes it's outgrowing people you thought would be in your life forever. And sometimes? It's realizing you were the flaky one. The distant one. The friend who didn't show up. (And that's a tough mirror to stand in front of.)
I've had friendships that saved me. And I've had friendships that shattered something in me.
And I've also had friendships that just... faded. Not because anyone did anything wrong, but because life got lifey. We changed. We grew - in different directions.
And still, I believe in it.

Even when I'm tired. Even when it hurts. Even when it's complicated. Because friendship is one of the few things in life that doesn't have to be perfect to be real. It can be messy and still be meaningful. It can take breaks and still be sacred. It can break your heart a little and still be worth the risk. So yes — this thing called friendship? I tire.

But I also love. I cherish. I grieve. I hope.
Because at the end of the day, life is hard enough. We need our people. Even if we have to find them again. Even if we have to become better at being one.
Friendship is having someone who gets your weird and stays anyway. It's a journey.

And sometimes the journey is bumpy, weird, overdue for a DTR (Define the Relationship), and full of voice notes that start with, "Hey, sorry I've been MIA but..."
But it's worth it. Still. Always.
Tired? Yes.
Done? Never.

Nathaniel Singbo shot I, OFF & FF, TFC Ikoyi Lagos, 2025

FFshot it, Beauty by him, Erin Ijesha, Nigeria, 2023

SILENCE IS LOUD.

Like... ear-splitting loud.
And not in the peaceful, spa music, birds-chirping, lavender-oil diffuser kind of way. No. Silence, real silence, the kind that wraps around your life like a thick fog: it's a whole experience. A season. A reckoning.
I think I'm in a season of silence. And honestly... It's hard.

No one warns you about this part; the part where everything goes quiet, where nothing seems to be moving, where God, the universe, your intuition, even your group chat... all feel like they've gone radio silent.

At first, it feels like punishment. Like, hello? Is this thing on? Did I miss the memo? But then you start to realize - silence isn't absence. It's presence, just wearing a different outfit. One with no subtitles, no background music, no notifications. Just... stillness.
We're not used to it!
We live in a world that worships noise: noise disguised as productivity, noise disguised as popularity, noise disguised as purpose.

We scroll, swipe, like, listen, respond, react, refresh.
We fill every quiet moment with something. Anything. Because stillness makes us confront things we've been running from in high resolution. But in the silence, the real, awkward, uncomfortable silence - things start to happen.

Things that don't make it to Instagram. You begin to hear yourself again. You start to notice where it hurts. Where you've been performing. Where you've been settling. You start to feel the grief you shoved into a corner. You start to dream again. You start to heal.

Silence is where you meet the parts of you that only speak in whispers. It's where growth happens quietly, secretly, like roots pushing deep underground. Nothing looks like it's changing on the outside, but you're being remade. It's also where you realize that sometimes, the reason you can't hear anything is because you're being taught to listen differently. Not with your ears, but with your soul.

With your patience. With your spirit. But let's be honest - silence is quirky too.
It has this weird way of making you suddenly want to clean your whole house at 2 a.m., cry during tv commercials and old movies, re-read old text messages from your phone just to feel something. It's like emotional detox. There are no distractions, so everything rises to the surface.

But here's the thing:
Silence isn't empty. It's full.
Full of answers, full of healing, full of direction - even if you can't see it yet.
It's the womb of reinvention. It's where you go to shed old skins and step into who you're becoming. And when you finally emerge? You won't be the same. You'll be softer. Sharper. Stronger. You'll speak with more intention. You'll walk with more clarity. You'll know what your own voice sounds like.

So yes - silence is loud.
But sometimes that's exactly what you need. Because when the world goes quiet, you finally start to hear yourself.
And wow... that voice?
She's been waiting for you.

SILENCE DIDN'T KNOCK.

It didn't ask for permission. It just arrived. Heavy, unfamiliar, uninvited.
But necessary.
I hated it at first. Hated the way it sat with me, made me face things I didn't want to see.
It wasn't peaceful. It wasn't calm. It was loud.
Louder than anything I've ever known. Louder than noise. Louder than words.
But here's the thing about silence:
It forces you to listen. To hear what's been buried. What's been tucked away in corners of your soul, covered in excuses, distractions, and busyness. It brings everything to the surface, even the stuff you never wanted to feel again.
And at first, I fought it. I ran from it, tried to fill the space with something - anything - because silence made me feel too much.

Too vulnerable. Too real.
But the more I fought, the louder it became. And somehow, in that painful, raw silence, I started to hear myself again. I started to hear what I needed to hear. The truth I had been avoiding. The clarity I had been too busy to see. The strength I had forgotten I had. I began to understand that silence isn't an absence.
It's a presence - a presence that clears your soul, washes the dust from your heart, and leaves you raw, refined, empowered.

And when I finally sat with it long enough, I realized that silence isn't empty. It's full. Full of the things that matter most. Full of the things that make you stronger. Braver. More alive.
It's scary, yeah. Painful, yes. But it's also beautiful.
It's the place where you stop pretending. Where you shed what doesn't serve you. Where you feel everything you've been running from. And still stand.

Now?
I welcome silence. I embrace it. I've learned that silence is not the absence of sound; It's the presence of truth. It's the space where I become whole. Where I refine, heal, and rise.
Silence is loud. But in its loudness, I find peace. I find clarity. I find myself.

F
E

WINGING IT

Some days, I wake up and think, "Here we go again... just winging it!"
No plans, no clue, just coffee in hand and hope in my heart.
I'm out here like a squirrel on espresso: all over the place, zooming around with zero direction, but at least I'm moving, right?
Life didn't come with a manual, so I'm over here just highlighting random chapters and hoping for the best.
And honestly?

I'm thriving in a "whoops, I forgot my keys" kind of way. Some people have a "game plan." I have a "let's see what happens" plan.
It's not pretty, but it's authentic: like wearing mismatched socks and still rocking it. Winging it is me saying, "This might go spectacularly wrong, but it might also not!" And that's all I really need.
If my life were any more planned out, I'd probably get bored and start napping.

So here's to winging it.
A little chaos.
A lot of coffee.
And the weird joy of not knowing what comes next.

FAITH & ACTION:
PRAYERS, PLANS, & A LITTLE ELBOW GREASE

FF shot it, He covers me, Benin Republic, 2024

Across

3. is patient and is kind

4. a thought or suggestion

7. showing reverence and devotion

9. how to end prayers

11. confident expectation and trust in God's promises and faithfulness

12. What happen you strike 2 stones

13. God's unmerited favour and love

Down

1. task or tasks to be undertaken

2. To stand up

5. process of doing something

6. bring (something) into existence

8. Evidence of things not seen

10. what to do all the time

AMEN - NOW GET UP

Let's be honest... I grew up hearing, "Just pray about it."
Pray about school. Pray about that job. Pray about that situationship (even though, deep down, you know the Holy Spirit already left the group chat 😄).
Pray, pray, pray.
And yes, prayer is powerful.
I believe in it with every fibre of my (slightly caffeinated) being.
But somewhere along the way, we got a little too comfortable stopping at the prayer part.

We pray, but do we plan?
We declare, but do we show up?
We lay hands, but do we lay bricks?

Even the Bible calls us out on this: "Faith without works is dead."- James 2:17
Imagine Moses praying at the Red Sea and refusing to stretch out his staff.
Imagine Noah praying for safety but never building the ark.
Imagine Esther praying for deliverance and saying, "You know what?
I'll just stay home today."
We wouldn't be quoting them; we'd be wondering, "What happened to that guy?"

Here's what I'm learning: faith is the spark, action is the firewood.
You can't roast your vision over an empty flame.
So yes, let's keep praying.
But then let's get up, drink some tea, open that laptop, write that pitch, show up for that idea, and move with God, not just talk to Him.

MORE THAN AMEN:
THE PRAYER + PLOUGH LIFE

In Nigeria, if prayer could solve everything, we'd all be billionaires with perfect roads, zero traffic, and 24/7 electricity.
We pray in churches, in buses, on voice notes, during meetings (even when we should be meeting). We decree, we declare, we scatter enemies. We know how to pray - loud, long, and with our full chest.
But here's the thing: prayer alone isn't the whole equation.
Yes, prayer changes things, but faith without action is just... wishful thinking in a religious outfit.

Even Jesus prayed and then He got to work. He didn't pray for fish and loaves and then sit there. He multiplied them and fed the people.
Nehemiah prayed about rebuilding Jerusalem... and then got bricks and people and sweat and strategy involved.
Ruth didn't just pray for provision: she got up and gleaned in the fields.

Even Paul - miracle-working, demon-chasing Paul - still made tents to support himself.
So... what are we doing after the "Amen"?
Because prayer is the fuel, not the finish line.
It aligns us, strengthens us, downloads wisdom.
But we still have to show up, respond to the call, and put our hands to the plough - and sometimes, also to the spreadsheet, the PowerPoint slide, the shovel, the sewing machine, the steering wheel, and the lecture room.
So how do we ensure our prayers are effective?
Pray with purpose, not panic. God's not moved by performance but by partnership.

Listen after you pray because sometimes the answer is, "Get up and go do it."
Ask for strategy, not just blessings. "Lord, give me wisdom to run this business," is better than "Lord, send me customers while I nap."
Be willing to be the answer to your own prayers. Sometimes God sends you.

Work like it's up to you. Pray like it's up to God. (Spoiler: It's both)
Look, prayer is powerful. Necessary. Beautiful.
But let's not hide behind it while the world passes by.
Prayer is the prep. Work is the proof. Faith is the fuel. Obedience is the "GO."

Let's build and pray. Dream and plan. Sow and speak.
And when people look at us, may they see not just a prayerful people but a fruitful one, too. Now excuse me, I need to go respond to that email I "prayed about" last week. 😄

P.S.: Miracles love momentum.

COLOUR AWAY

JUST A WHISPER

It's not always thunder, not fire, not flame
Sometimes it's a whisper
That still speaks His name.
It's hands in the dishes, a sigh in the rain,
A pause in the chaos, that carries His name.
It's not just in churches, or kneeling at night,
It's found in the moments, we choose what is right.
It's talking and listening, it's silence and song,
It's knowing He's with me, all the day long.
So I breathe and I mumble, some days I just stare,
But He hears me still.
That, my friend, is prayer.

HERE IS HOLY

"Take off your sandals, for the place where you are standing is holy ground." – Exodus 3:5
Okay, Lord.
Let's talk.
I'm currently sitting in a hoodie that's older than some of my friendships, sipping lukewarm tea that tastes like procrastination, and wearing one sock, just one, because the other has, once again, disappeared into the mysterious sock abyss. And You're telling me this is holy?

This? This moment where I haven't brushed my hair, I've got three open snack wrappers next to me, and I just accidentally sent a thumbs-up to my boss in response to a serious email? (Why, thumbs-up emoji, why?!)
And yet... I hear You.
You whisper, "Here is holy."
Not "after I get my act together" holy.
Not "once I've read Leviticus without zoning out" holy.
Not "when I stop using sarcasm as a spiritual gift" holy.
Just... here.

Right now.
In my undone, half-baked, multitasking mess of a Monday.
Because You're not waiting for me at the end of a 5-day devotional streak. You're not holding holiness hostage behind an early morning prayer and perfectly highlighted Bible.

You're right here.
In the silence between my chaotic thoughts. In the patience it takes not to snap at someone who clearly deserves it. In my offering of folding laundry like it's an act of worship (and let's be real, sometimes it is).
I used to think holiness looked like burning bushes and angelic choirs. Now I think it might look like showing up for people who wouldn't do the same. Like choosing compassion over passive-aggressive Instagram stories. Like forgiving without needing an audience or a dramatic exit speech. Like not sending that shady text I drafted but never sent. (Growth!)

Maybe the fire isn't outside; maybe it's in me.
Maybe holiness isn't a location: it's a posture.
A quiet awareness that You're already here, even in the socks-and-snacks version of my life.

So Lord, help me remember:
It doesn't have to be picture-perfect to be sacred.
The divine shows up in dishes, in awkward Zoom silences, team meetings, and in that nudge to pray instead of panic.

Holiness might look like me, tired but trying, loving but learning, showing up when I'd rather hide under a blanket (preferably with the A.C. blasting).
This is holy ground. This unfiltered, unedited, slightly unhinged life of mine.
And You? You're in it with me.
Amen.

From FF's lens Waterfalls, Erin Ijesha, Nigeria 2023

Music
dance

WALKING IN THE RHYTHM OF WORSHIP

I walk in the rhythm of worship, not just swaying to a tune,
But in brushing my teeth while praying, and losing socks by noon.
Not just on holy mountains, sometimes in laundry heaps,
Where worship looks like "Jesus, please... I need more than just sleep."
It's spreading joy like butter: thick and slightly extra,
Laughing at bad puns, and yes, dancing like a Pentecostal T-Rex.

I worship when I hold the door, or lend an awkward hug,
And when I say "I'm fine," but I'm really one spill from a shrug.
I'm vulnerable, not fragile, more like a soft avocado,
Trying to ripen gracefully, but sometimes... it's a no-go.

I cry and then I giggle, I stumble, but I pray,
"Lord, could You work through this hot mess and still bless folks today?"
I ask God to lead me daily, like a GPS for life,
Though I still miss turns, detour in pride, and argue like He's my wife.

But He reroutes with mercy, like "Recalculating, sweet child."
And I'm back on track with grace, even if it takes a while.
I try to serve with purpose, not just 'cause it's a rule,
But because love looks like dishes done, or picking kids up from school.
It's choosing peace in traffic (okay, trying 'cos let's be real),
It's "Jesus, take the wheel," but also "Jesus, please refill..."

This worship ain't a Sunday suit, it's sweatpants and a sigh,
It's when I show up empty, but still choose to give faith a try.
It's telling folks about Jesus, not with drama, but with love, food, and tales of good things.
And hoping grace covers all the times I talked too much... or lacked.

So no, I don't just worship when music is playing or the choir starts singing
I do it when I choose to love, when I say "yes" to the Lord.
Through jokes, through tears, through "Lord, I don't know what I'm doing!"
He says, "That's okay, just keep moving, I'll keep the rhythm brewing."

PAIN

There are days when pain feels so raw, it's like my whole body is on fire. I can feel it in my chest, my stomach - it's like it's consuming me from the inside out. I don't even have to try: it's just there, pulsing, like a reminder that something isn't right. I can't shake it. I can't run from it. And when it's that intense, all I want to do is hide from it, ignore it, pretend it's not happening. But no matter how much I try to push it away, it's there. It's always there, like a shadow I can't escape.

And then, there are the other days. The ones when I don't even know what I'm feeling. I don't know if it's sadness or anger or something else entirely. It's just this dull ache — not sharp, but deep. Like I'm walking through a fog, and I can't quite catch my breath. I don't have the words for it, and I don't know how to make sense of it. It's just this overwhelming weight that doesn't scream, but quietly lingers, making everything feel a little heavier than it should.

But here's the thing I've realized: as much as I hate pain, I'm grateful for it, too. It's such a strange thing to say, but I've learned that feeling pain, however hard it is, is a sign that I'm alive. I'm not numb. I'm not pretending everything is fine when it's not. And maybe that's the part I've come to understand. Pain means I'm living, I'm growing, even when it feels like I'm breaking. It means I'm still here, still trying, still fighting.

There's power in pain. I've felt it. It has a way of reshaping you, whether you want it to or not. It bends you, it molds you. Some days it feels like it's going to destroy you, but it doesn't. You come out of it a little cracked, but stronger. More resilient. More aware of yourself.

But managing pain? That's been a whole other journey. There are days when I feel like I'm barely holding it together, trying not to let it swallow me whole. On other days, I've learned to just sit with it, let it wash over me, and not be afraid of it. I've realized the only way to get through it is to feel it, let it run its course, and trust that it won't last forever. That's the thing with pain: it has a way of fading, leaving room for healing to take its place.

It's tough. There's no denying that. But what I've learned is that pain isn't the end of the story. It doesn't define me. What defines me is how I rise from it. How I choose to keep going, even when I feel like I can't. How I choose to learn from it and grow, and maybe, just maybe, how I allow myself to be a little softer, a little more open, because I've been through the fire and survived.

So, yeah. Pain is heavy. But it's also powerful. It teaches me things I didn't know I needed to learn. And in the end, I come out the other side, not just surviving, but learning how to live more fully.

I worship. The Cathedral, Luxembourg 2025. Sholto Fraser

MY FATHER'S DAUGHTER

Some days the world feels too heavy,
Like I'm carrying more than I can handle.
But then I remember: I am my Father's daughter.
And He's not just any father. He's the One who lifts
me when I fall, who whispers peace when my heart
races.

I don't have to figure it all out, because I'm safe in
His love, safe in His arms.
I don't have to be perfect. I don't have to be
anything I'm not.

He loves me as I am, with all my mess, with all my
mistakes.
And in that love, I find strength to keep going.
I'm never alone. I'm never too far gone.
I am His, and that makes all the difference

COVERED BY THE MOST HIGH

I've been thinking a lot lately. About people. About who I've surrounded myself with and whether they're the ones who will lift me up when the weight of the world feels too heavy. The thing is, the world can feel like a lot sometimes — chaotic, draining, and unpredictable. But even in the chaos, I know I'm covered by the Most High. That's the foundation of my peace.

Still, it's not just about me and God, is it? It's about the people I allow into my life, the ones who walk with me through the highs and lows. Have I created a circle that reflects His grace, His love, His strength? Have I surrounded myself with people who will pull me up when I'm sinking, and laugh with me when I'm soaring?

There are times when I've had to step back and evaluate the people around me. Some bring light, love, and laughter. Others? Well, let's just say they remind me of how not to be. The energy you keep matters. I know I need people who will remind me that I'm not in this alone. People who are strong when I'm weak, and gentle when I'm struggling. I need people who reflect grace, the kind of grace that covers all my imperfections without judgment.

But I also know it's not just about being surrounded by the right people. It's about being the right person, too. I have to be someone who shows up for others, just like they show up for me. It's a two-way street. The love, the strength, the grace: it has to flow both ways.

As I sit with these thoughts, I realize that the people I've chosen to keep close are a reflection of God's love for me. They're not perfect, but they bring me strength when I'm tired, grace when I fall short, and love when I forget to love myself. I'm learning that it's not just about being covered by God, it's about being covered by those He places in my life. Together, we carry each other's burdens, and in doing so, we all get a little stronger.

So yes, I've been blessed. I am covered, not only by the Most High, but by a circle that reflects His grace and love. And that makes all the difference.

CHURCH GIRL, NOT SUPERWOMAN

Don't get me wrong - I'm not complaining.
I love being a church girl.
There's something beautiful about it: the worship, the community, the "God bless you, sister!" at the door that somehow warms your soul even when NEPA has taken light.
But phew. Sometimes... I just need a minute.

Because the truth is, while I'm saying "Yes, Lord" with one hand, the other hand is holding three church group chats, a to-do list for Sunday, a contribution list for Pastor's birthday, and the lingering question: "Did I even pray for myself today?"
It's like this constant tug-of-war: wanting to be fully present, fully surrendered, but also... just fully okay.

I love God. I love His house.
 But sometimes, I feel like I'm being pulled in eleven directions at once, and none of them are giving clear instructions.
You serve. You give. You show up.
And you're supposed to do it joyfully, gracefully, and preferably without eye bags or burnout.

And let's not talk about the guilt.
Because when you do feel tired, or overwhelmed, or like maybe, just maybe, you want to take a breather, it's like:
"Oh wow, you're losing your fire?"
No o, I'm just losing my sanity. Slightly.
And I get it. We're not here to be comfortable, we're here to be transformed.

But transformation is hard when you're running on spiritual fumes and trying to be all things to all people.
Also, small confession: I sometimes wonder how pastors do it.
Like, are you okay? Blink twice for help.
Because if this is what leadership-lite feels like, then the full package must come with free holy endurance oil.
But really, I think what I'm wrestling with is this:
How do I serve God wholeheartedly without losing me in the process?
Because I don't exist in a vacuum.

There's life. Work. Family. Pressure.
All these forces colliding, trying to be the "good leader," the "good Christian," the "kind, smiling, Spirit-filled, always-available vessel of God."
And sometimes, in all that doing, I feel like I'm... drowning a little.
Like I'm showing up in every room except the quiet one where it's just me and God, no titles, no tasks, just presence.
But I'm learning.

Learning that He never asked me to carry it all.
Learning that being "church girl" doesn't mean being "Superwoman."
Learning that grace isn't just what I give, it's what I need too.
So yes, I'm still here.

Still loving God. Still loving church.
Still showing up, but now with boundaries, breath, and a little more softness for myself.
Because I'm not trying to burn out for Jesus.
I want to burn bright for Him — for a long, long time.

STILL ON PURPOSE

You looked for purpose like a distant flame,
As if it hides behind a title or name.
But while you waited for a sign from above,
Purpose walked with you, quiet like love.
You prayed for more, yet you were already placed
In the lives you touch, in the steps you trace.
What feels like silence is often a seed,
What feels like loneliness is actually leading.

Leading doesn't always shout or shine,
Sometimes it's staying when others decline.
Faith doesn't flirt with easy applause,
It holds the line for a higher cause.
So don't despise the day you're in,
The fight, the fire, the daily spin.
God's purpose isn't far or vague -
It's you, alive, in motion, brave.

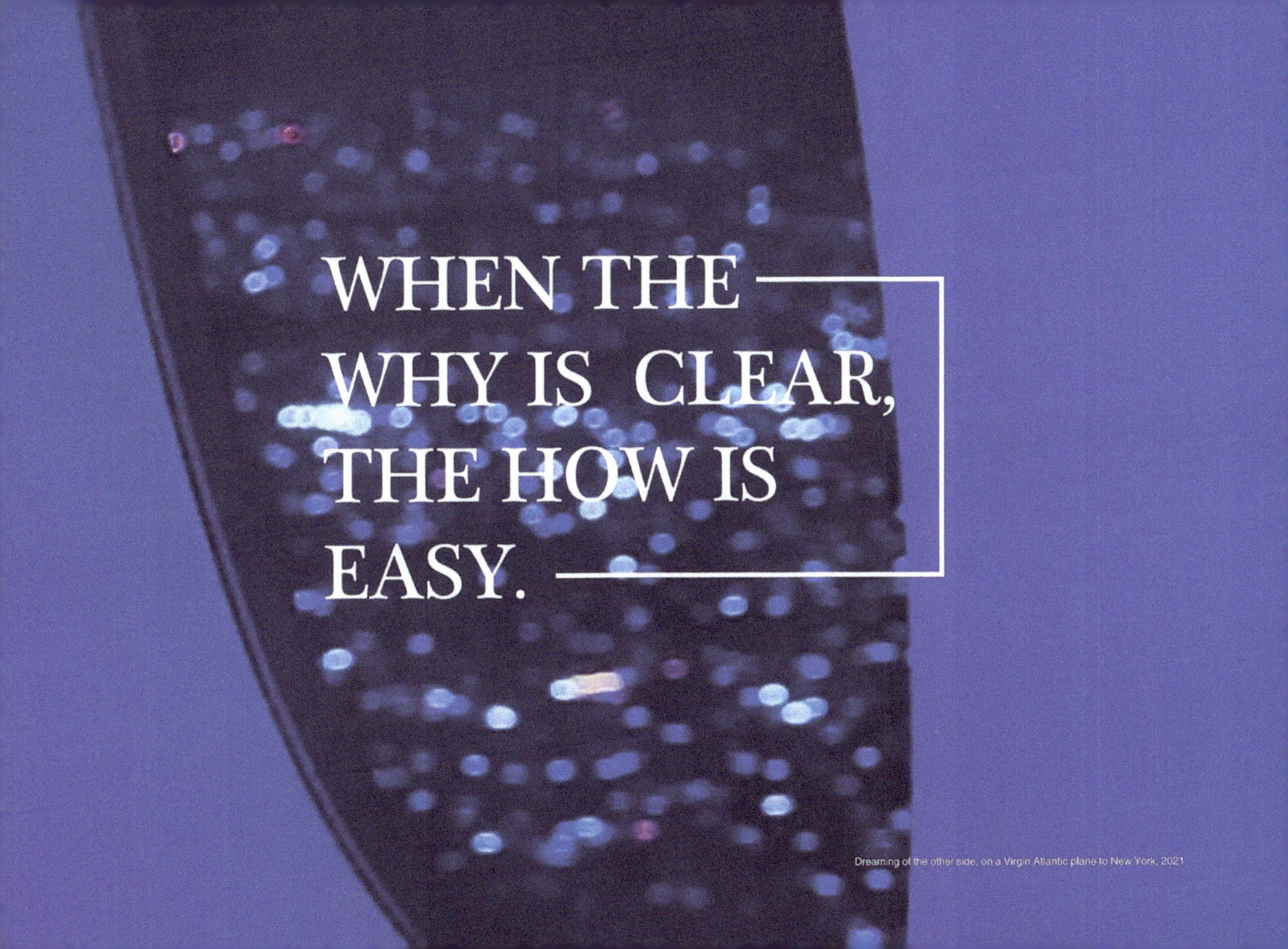

Dreaming of the other side, on a Virgin Atlantic plane to New York, 2021

MY WEALTH CAME *with* JOY

NOT TO MAKE ME BOAST, BUT TO TEACH ME DEEPER HUMILITY

AN ODE TO LIFE

You came into this world like a sunrise, soft, golden, and full of promise.
You were named "my wealth has come" and oh, did you live up to it.
You didn't just bring wealth, you were joy wrapped in sass, sweetness, and the kind of laughter that echoed in the soul.

You were a light that danced through our lives, kind to your core, bold in ways that made me proud, and funny. Lord, so funny, with a wit that could floor me mid-sentence and stories that somehow always turned into giggles. Even in the hardest moments, you made room for laughter. We laughed about everything, didn't we?

Even sickness didn't stand a chance against your sense of humor.
You dreamed big, not in loud, showy ways, but with a quiet fire that said, "I'm here. I matter. I've got things to do."
And you did them, even when the pain tried to steal your breath.
You kept showing up. Kept loving. Kept fighting.
You were soft and steel at the same time.
I still don't know how you did it.
You taught me so much.
About courage. About joy.

About how to sit in the dark and still believe in the morning. And about the power of a well-timed eye roll when someone was being extra. You were a masterclass in grace with edge.

To love you was the easiest thing, a delight I'll never take for granted.
To know you was to be reminded that life isn't about how long you're here,
but how deeply you live while you are.

My niece, my girl, my unexpected teacher, my joy.
I miss you in all the little places: in stories I wish I could tell you,
in jokes that aren't as funny without your laugh, in songs that sound like you, and in quiet moments when I swear I can feel you smiling.
You lived with love.
You left with love.
And you left it all with us.
And that joy?
It's still here.
You brought it.
You are it. Forever.
Thank You Olamide

ACKNOWLEDGEMENTS:

For FAM & Alero,
the steady voice, the soul-whisperers, the ones who've been holding space for my words
long before they made it to paper. Your wisdom has been a quiet lighthouse on stormy seas.

For Alex & Akinbayo
the fresh wind, the spark, the gentle reminder that youth can carry depth, and poise can carry joy.
Watching you has taught me as much as listening to you.

For The friends
you rock.

You all showed up in different seasons, but with the same unshakable belief in me.
This book carries your fingerprints and your faith.
Thank you for showing up, for staying, and for being part of this becoming.

And to my husband,
for pretending to understand poetry,
and for loving me anyway.

ABBA
Thank you, I love you

ACTION PLAN

GOAL	WHY	MOTIVATION	START DATE
			DEADLINE

OBSTACLES	RESOURCES	NOTE

BIG STEPS	LITTLE STEPS	